BOUQUET

BOUQUET

Twelve Flower Fables
by Myrna Davis

Paintings by Paul Davis

Clarkson N. Potter, Inc./Publishers

NEW YORK

DISTRIBUTED BY CROWN PUBLISHERS, INC.

Published by Clarkson N. Potter, Inc.
One Park Avenue
New York, New York 10016

Published simultaneously in Canada
by General Publishing Company Limited

Manufactured in Japan

**Library of Congress Cataloging in Publication
Data**

Davis, Myrna.
  Bouquet: twelve flower fables.

   1. Fables, American.   2. Flowers—Fiction.
I. Davis, Paul, 1938–   . II. Title.
PS3554.A9373B6   1982   813′.54   81-17300
                                            AACR2
ISBN: 0-517-546043

10 9 8 7 6 5 4 3 2 1

First Edition

For John and Matthew

Contents

Acknowledgments

The paintings in this book were first shown at the Nishimura Gallery in Tokyo, and we are grateful to Chieko and Kenji Nishimura for their generous assistance.

Special thanks go also to Joan Meisel for researching material; to Concetta Clarke, director of the Bridgehampton Library, for her help; and to Robert Gerbereux, director of the Southampton College Library, for permission to use the John Steinbeck Room, where part of the book was written.

Finally, we want to express our appreciation to Carol Southern for her thoughtful work as editor.

Preface

"The force that through the green fuse drives the flower, drives my green age . . . ," wrote Dylan Thomas. To look more than glancingly upon flowers is to begin an inquiry into the essential mysteries of life. Reproduction is their ordained province, and attendant on them are questions of death and rebirth, growth and decay, pleasure and nourishment, beauty and desire.

Confucius numbered the cultivation of flowers as one of the arts necessary to a civilized human being, and an old Chinese proverb advises, "If you have two loaves of bread, sell one and buy a hyacinth." Neolithic artisans stamped flower images into clay cereal pots ten thousand years ago, and depictions of flowers exist in five-thousand-year-old frescoes of the palace of Knossos on Crete and in the carved wall of the temple of Karnak in Egypt. More than sixty thousand years ago a grieving Neanderthal laced twelve different kinds of flowers into a funeral litter. Every known culture has included flowers in their rites and celebrations, and many have woven them into their myths.

Two of the tales in this collection, "Consolation, the Poppy" and "Healing, the Peony," are adapted from Greek and Roman myths. "Sincerity, the Lily" is based on an early Christian legend; "Steadfastness, the Camellia" on a Chinese legend; "Magnificence, the Orchid" on a legend from the Philippines; and "Optimism, the Chrysanthemum" on a Japanese fairy tale. For "Eloquence, the Iris," the idea to juxtapose the flower with an excerpt from the Egyptian *Book of the Dead* was inspired by a caption under a nineteenth-century illustration of the Sphinx, in which the ornament on its head was identified as an iris. In "Secrecy, the Rose" and "Thought, the Pansy," imaginary characters inhabit a biblical time and place; "Passion, the Tulip" concerns an imaginary couple in a historical event. The central incident in "Treachery, the Dahlia" is invented, but the circumstances and the people are not. "Wisdom, the Lotus" is a retelling of a Zen parable I heard once long ago.

The titles of the fables are qualities the flowers were accorded in the popular Victorian "language of flowers." Lady Mary Wortley Montague, an eighteenth-century Englishwoman living in Turkey, wrote to friends of a poetic art she had discovered there, a language for lovers in which everyday objects were used to convey messages. In the next century this delightful concept caught the imagination of the English, focusing exclusively on flowers, whole volumes being devoted to the elucidation of their symbolic characteristics. Recipients of bouquets studied each blossom for its intended meaning.

This book was conceived as a "bouquet" of stories and paintings, a gift from the heart. If flowers remind us of fundamental matters, we hope our offering will do no less.

MYRNA DAVIS

Secrecy

THE ROSE

Mishael ben Ezra no longer considered himself a lustful man. His blood had long cooled, he was faithful to his wife with ease, and his days were gratified by the adventures of trade. In the conduct of his business, the merchant had traveled throughout the known world. Yet of all the wonders he had seen, none surpassed those of his own city. Each time he returned from a journey and glimpsed the walls of Babylon from afar, his pulse quickened. Entering the famed Ishtar gate, its walls gleaming with ferocious images of dragons, bulls, and lions, he congratulated himself on being a man able to share in such grandeur.

Among the thousands of merchants of the city, ben Ezra was distinguished for his honesty, his perspicacity, and his resourcefulness in obtaining what was wanted. His trusted reputation had brought him, finally, to the palace of Belshazzar himself. Here, in the king's gardens, which were suspended on balconies high over the city, he negotiated pearls and silks, ivories and incense from the Orient, fine linens and wines, oils and dyes from the Mediterranean. His prices were dear but not unconscionably so, his patience boundless. The members of the royal party rolled their eyes in indignation. They threatened to dismiss him and send for another merchant, but ben Ezra remained unmoved. He calculated accurately the value of his wares and services to his clients, and at length his terms were accepted.

At midday it was said to be so hot on the streets of Babylon that a lizard might bake to death while crossing the road. Ben Ezra lingered in the uncommon cool of the palace gardens, verdant with trees and flowers. He regarded the Temple of Marduk in the distance with awe, its many-hued ziggurat rising like steps into the sun, and wondered if his own god, Jehovah, could contend with such unassailable power as was attributed to the king of all the Babylonian gods.

When the day relinquished some of its heat, ben Ezra prepared to leave. As he made his way down the long flights of stairs, something caught at his robe. Seeing that a rose had entangled itself in the fabric of his sleeve, the dutiful husband plucked the flower and slipped it into his water jar as a souvenir for his wife.

By the time he reached his house, in a far corner of the city, it was dark, and the rhythm of his wife's breathing told him she was asleep. Without lighting the oil lamp he undressed and lay next to her. The rose perfumed the air; in the moonlight it suggested a woman's face. Ben Ezra reached out to caress its silken petals, and against his fingers it assumed the shape of a woman. "Mishael," it sang, "I am Bibiya."

Moving softly alongside him, Bibiya brushed her arms, her thighs, the buds of her breasts against the body of ben Ezra. Her naked skin was like the petals of the rose; he stiffened with longing and fear. Still his wife slept. At length he plunged himself into the apparition. Her beckoning eyes glittered in the moonlight. "Bibiya," he murmured, pressing his lips upon her fragrant hair.

In the morning Mishael ben Ezra's wife greeted him warmly, inquiring after his health and the success of his visit to the palace. The rose stood sparkling in the water jar. He was relieved; his adultery had been a dream. He decided, however, not to present the flower to his wife.

The next night ben Ezra lay awake longer than usual. He waited for his wife's breathing to slow and grow deep. He stroked the wiry hairs on his chest, the smooth tiles of the floor, the coarse wool of the carpet that lay upon it. He listened in the silence and then turned to the rose. Once more Bibiya appeared at his fingertips. This time Mishael ben Ezra did not hesitate. He did not question. He simply loved this woman of the rose and felt himself grow younger within her. Their motions of ecstasy did not disturb the marriage bed.

Each morning ben Ezra filled the jar with fresh water. His wife detected a tenderness in the act that she could attribute only to some mellowing of middle age. She once tried to touch the rose but was pricked by one of its thorns. She would have ignored it thereafter but ben Ezra, called away to the shores of the Euphrates asked her to care for it in his absence.

It took time for the merchant to arrange for the porters and donkeys necessary to transport the goods back to Babylon, and several nights passed, during which ben Ezra could think of little else but his rose. So distracted was he upon reaching Babylon that he failed to notice the shadowy groups of men digging with picks near the city's walls.

He hurried straight to the palace, anxious to deliver the wares and return home, but a feast was in progress and he was forced to wait. As the revelry increased with each passing hour, ben Ezra's patience dwindled, and when the new day dawned, he left abruptly, all obligations abandoned. He desired nothing any longer but Bibiya.

Arriving home, the merchant rushed past his wife to the water jar, but in its place he found only scattered clay fragments and rivulets of water drying on the floor. The rose of Babylon lay lifeless among them.

A short while later the news spread that the city had been taken during the previous night by Cyrus, the great Persian conqueror. The reign of Belshazzar was ended. While the unsuspecting king and his court celebrated, Cyrus's men had succeeded in diverting the waters of the moat surrounding the city and had made their way under the walls through the drained bed into Babylon's very heart. By the time the invaders were discovered, it was too late. Mishael ben Ezra and his wife fled the city. They continued, in their way, to love each other, and the merchant never spoke of the irreclaimable splendors of Babylon, or those of his Bibiya.

Magnificence

THE ORCHID

T agali's poisoned arrow inexplicably missed its target, the heart of General Lope de García, giving credence to the native chieftain's suspicion that Spaniards had no hearts at all. How else explain the ruthlessness with which these tight-lipped invaders had subjugated a gentle and gracious people?

When the great-masted galleons of Spain first sailed onto the Philippine horizon in 1564, the islanders of Luzon welcomed them with friendly expectation. Freely they offered their skills in weaving and metalworking, in fishing and raising livestock. The women, tall and strong and handsomely arrayed, danced and sang to the *kudayapi*, an instrument not unlike the Spaniards' guitar. At peace and proud, the islanders were ready to share what they had with the newcomers.

But the visitors had not come to be entertained or instructed. They were purposeful in their greed and in their belief that their ways were superior to any others on earth. Arrogantly they took what they wanted and destroyed what they did not. In desperation Tagali attempted to murder one of the oppressors who had so coldly betrayed his people's trust, and he failed. Apprehended and bound, he was thrown at his intended victim's feet. No in-

5

terpreter was needed to explain the general's angry directive. Tagali was to be put to death at once. With a sweep of his gloved hand, Lope de García ordered the condemned man away.

During this confrontation, the general's young wife, although sitting nearby, seemed oblivious, her attention absorbed by an unusual flower cupped in her hands. Its bizarre markings and shapes tantalized her, suggesting something more animal than plant. First its parts seemed to declare themselves as vagina, vulva, and clitoris, the womb itself. Then they appeared to be a penis and scrotum, perhaps also a tongue. She exclaimed involuntarily over this erotic allure.

Tagali saw her rapture. He called out to her that the flower she held was an orchid, and that he could bring her hundreds even more lovely if his execution might be stayed for one day. The señora, surprising herself, acted quickly. In the few weeks she had lived on the island, she had observed the Philippine women moving as equals among their men, rather than in the subservient manner she had been taught was appropriate for members of her sex. Their confident bearing and manners set an example of which she was quite unaware until the moment Tagali appealed to her, and she found herself interceding on his behalf.

His wife's boldness took Lope de García by surprise. Seldom did she ask for anything, and since joining him had seemed dispirited and preoccupied. Seeing her cheeks flush with color and her eyes brighten, he could not refuse her. He agreed but sent along ten armed guards to forestall any escape, and demanded he

© 1979 Paul Davis

return by the same hour the following day.

Tagali scoured the island for his ransom. He pulled giant orchids with two-foot long petals from the trees, and picked others, tinier than fingernails, from the undersides of rocks. He found them in marshes, near volcanoes, beside lakes and on vines. So many variations of this one species did he gather that were there no other flowers on earth they alone might satisfy the most avid student of botany.

The next afternoon, at the agreed hour, captive and captors emerged from the rain forest into the clearing of the Spanish camp. They came festooned with the most beguiling profusion of blossoms imaginable, some of which mimicked in appearance other wildlife, such as butterflies, birds, even fish. One by one they approached the señora, spilling their opulent bouquets before her. She thought the orchids were as dazzling as any jewels, the more precious for the evanescence, and that the muscles of Tagali's body, gleaming with perspiration, far outshone the golden helmets adorning her husband and his soldiers.

Lope de García did not wish to lose, indeed he wished to take credit for, the pleasure reflected on the face of his wife. Staying the execution, the general returned Tagali to freedom on the day they set sail for Spain. As the señora took a last look at the receding shore, she knew that the island's real treasures had been left behind.

Treachery

THE DAHLIA

Napoleon was in full retreat. He had, after seven years of marriage, insisted upon separate bedrooms, and Josephine's entreaties to the contrary had been of no avail. As the general's career progressed, great numbers of ladies, many of them young, pretty, and clever, stood willing to divert him. He was six years his wife's junior, and although she still appeared young, having been described by a contemporary as one of those women who "stay at thirty for fifteen years," Josephine felt like one of her own cut flowers, about to be replaced even before she had begun to fade. Her stratagems to hold her husband's attention grew increasingly reckless.

Botany was her passion, Bonaparte aside, and in its service she supported some of the most notable gardeners and naturalists on the continent. The gardens of Malmaison, the Bonaparte estate, were already famous. A new acquisition was the dahlia, at that time a great rarity in Europe, having only recently arrived from Mexico by way of Spain.

One night Josephine meant to use the flower to surprise the general. She ordered her gardeners to deliver to her apartments twenty dozen full-blown dahlias, in preparation for Napoleon's

visit later that evening. If the profusion of those flowers strewn on the empress's bed puzzled her ladies-in-waiting, they were too circumspect to comment, accustomed as they were to their mistress's indulgences. She owned upwards of eight hundred dresses, nearly as many pairs of shoes, and even more pairs of gloves. Sufficient sets of silk stockings and lace undergarments to change three times a day overflowed her wardrobe, and if it had pleased her to sleep on a few hundred rare flowers, well, such were the prerogatives of royalty, and nothing compared to the extravagances of the *ancien régime*.

Bathed, powdered, combed, and perfumed, Josephine dismissed her attendants and set about arranging herself artfully on the great canopied bed, covering herself with nothing more than these lavish blooms, the lush peach color like her skin. Her husband, certain to be charmed by the originality of her seduction, would be hers tonight.

But no familiar footfall muted the ticking of the vermeil clock atop the marble mantel. Josephine waited, motionless as the gentlemen and ladies framing the clock's face, while the hands moved across the Roman numerals: ten, eleven, twelve. Her hopes wilted with the petals. Chilled by disappointment, she shook herself free of the flowers and slipped forlornly between the imperial linens.

Waking the next morning in a litter of dead dahlias, Josephine was overcome by superstitious dread. As she watched the blossoms being swept up, now withered and pale, they recalled to her the guillotined heads of a decade earlier, among them that of her first husband, Alexandre de Beauharnais. The flowers reminded her also of herself, an unlucky tropical transplant on French soil. She had grown up on the island of Martinique, half-believing in voodoo. Now she feared that her fate would be that of the dahlias, so carelessly used and discarded.

It was not long before Napoleon began to broach openly the idea of separation, and within a few years he divorced his once-adored Josephine. Taking refuge at Malmaison, the former empress retired from social life and devoted herself to her burgeoning gardens. She reportedly became especially possessive of her dahlias.

Thought

THE PANSY

Gilles of Anjou lay on the stone floor of the great Cathedral of Our Lady of Chartres and tried to sleep. He had made the exhausting pilgrimage because of stories he had heard of miracles attesting to the Virgin's presence there, and he wanted to fulfill his part of a bargain made with her in faraway Damascus. She had brought him safely out of that terrible battlefield of the Third Crusade, and now he was prepared to do whatever she might ask.

It might be said that during the Middle Ages the Holy Mother nearly eclipsed her Son, for whatever judgment might be pronounced on a sinner by God could be commuted by her intercession. This merciful recourse lightened the burdens of those years. So loved was Mary by the people of France, so real was she to them, that they erected dozens of cathedrals and hundreds of churches to her within the span of a single century. Of them all, Chartres was truly the most glorious. Inspired in a great wave of enthusiasm after the First Crusade, artisans and craftsmen created a palace worthy of the Queen of Heaven on earth. When Gilles saw it for the first time, no doubt it remained in his mind that she herself was resident there and would receive his prayers.

During the night, Gilles was disturbed by a deep, pounding reverberation, which seemed to come from beneath the stones. He rose to his feet uncertainly, impelled to find its source. Following the sound, he was led through a nearby wood into a vast clearing, where he saw hundreds, perhaps thousands, of men and women silhouetted against the sky, gathered in solemn ceremony. Gilles knew they were the ancient Druids, priests and priestesses of Gaul, speaking in their forgotten tongue. There were the leaders of the Tricassi, the Parisii, the Turones, the Lemovices, those tribes who long ago had inhabited places that inherited their names: Troyes, Paris, Tours, Limoges; the Pictones of Poitiers, the Redones of Rennes, the Andecavi of his own Anjou, and not last, the Carnutes of Chartres. This place was the site of their greatest assemblies.

It was the sixth night of the moon, whose waxing influence was wanted for the proceedings. A threat from Rome had drawn the Druids to this sacred grove for divine guidance. To those whose name was taken from the Greek word for tree, *drus,* trees embodied powerful gods. Mistletoe, which seemed to nourish itself magically on air alone, had been found on rare oak. It was an omen. One white-robed priest climbed the tree, a sickle of bronze at his side, while another led two snow-white bulls to the spot beneath the mistletoe. As the coveted parasite was cut down from its aerie, the throats of the bulls were slit. Blood ran black as ink in the moonlight, staining the white hides, the white robes, the white violets underfoot.

© 1979 Paul Davis

In the entrails of the slaughtered animals portents were read. There would be war with Caesar, and transformation in the shape of a cross. It was agreed, then, to support a rebellion against the Romans under one of their chieftains, Vercingetorix. They would burn their towns before the advancing enemy. What had been written in blood would be executed in fire. As the ancient forebears of France raised their torches, their chants rolled through the woods like thunder. Gilles made his way back to the cathedral, the sting of smoke in his nostrils.

If what he had witnessed was a dream or vision, what Gilles saw next was real enough. Some time during the night a fire had started in the apse, and billows of smoke poured from the burning oak beams high above the heads of the sleeping pilgrims. Rousing them with shouts, Gilles ran into the streets of the town calling for help. Men, women, and children, the sturdy and the infirm, responded to his alarm. Peasants and noblemen bowed themselves under the same yokes to carry water, laboring through the night to save the palace of their beloved Mary. The edifice, though damaged greatly, was saved.

As Gilles knelt to give thanks to his Queen, he noticed in the numinous wreckage small violets growing, their petals marked as if with stains of blood. They suggested to him little wizened faces, semblances of those ancestors lost a thousand years before. Gilles picked some of the flowers his countrymen called *pensées,* or pansies, for "thoughts," and laid them on her altar. Then he kept one himself, and set out at last for home.

Consolation

THE POPPY

Proserpine was enchanted by the gossamer morning. Birds wafted overhead, chattering and chirping, making nests for spring. She lay on her back and studied the intense color of the sky. Was it opaque or transparent? She could not tell. The few wisps of cloud that appeared quickly dissipated in the corrosive blue. She jumped up and laughed, whirling until her soft skirts rippled around her, then stopped abruptly, the horizon spinning dizzily and teetering to a halt like the toy tops of her childhood.

A bouquet was in order for this day. As she wandered among the bright wildflowers, inspecting this one, choosing that, a viper's bugloss caught her interest. It stood out from the others, its petals a shade deeper than the sky, the tiny hairs on its stem glistening in the sun. She reached out, hesitant; it was at once enticing and loathsome. As she stood there, she felt the hairs on her own neck rise, as if someone were watching her. Turning, she shielded her eyes against Phoebus's bright chariot now high in the heavens and was startled to see the dark, tall figure of a man.

His presence was commanding. More excited than afraid, she met his gaze and was hypnotized, as a small prey by its predator.

17

His black pupils widened and he held out his hand. Surprising herself with reckless acquiescence, she took his hand in her own. Then the meadow disappeared, the crystalline light shattered into a million fragments, and everything was blackness.

The earth truly opened, it is told, and swallowed the couple whole. This fervent suitor of Proserpine was none other than Pluto himself, god of the underworld. At the very moment that Proserpine had felt most alive in her young life, the lord of the dead had espied her and desired her for his bride. She offered no resistance, perhaps because of her inexperience or because, as the daughter of Ceres, the earth goddess, and of Jove, god of gods, she had anticipated an uncommon destiny. The ardor of her abductor aroused her own. As the two made their unremitting descent into Pluto's realm, however, Proserpine grew frightened at the absence of light, and wondered whether the radiance of their passion could compensate for eternal darkness.

When her daughter did not come home that evening, Ceres was distressed. She walked back and forth along the paths she knew Proserpine to frequent, and then set out through the Sicilian countryside, from house to house, village to village, questioning everyone. Weeks, months, passed. Ceres grew haggard, her clothes dirty and torn; worse, she was neglecting her agricultural duties. Crops died, leaves fell from the trees and crumbled to dust, seeds lay inert in the ground. People used up what stores of food they had, and babies cried in hunger.

The other gods became concerned. It was possible that all hu-

© 1979 Paul Davis

manity might perish if something were not done to bring Ceres to her senses. They thought if Ceres were told of Proserpine's fate she would give up her search and tend the earth again. But the news only compounded her grief with rage, and the anguished mother persisted, angrily demanding that her daughter be restored to her.

Somnus, the god of sleep, had a plan. Ceres was exhausted; if he could find a means to make her rest, she then might be receptive to reason. By the time the goddess reached the summit of Mount Etna, his trap was laid. As Ceres ignited two torches in the volcano's fires to aid her in her quest, she looked about her, and in the flickering light saw thousands of flowers with paper-thin petals, their colors like stained glass. These were poppies, created by Somnus to divert her. Their aroma, bitter as her sorrow, pervaded the air. As she picked one, her fingernail pierced its pod, and a milky liquid seeped out, numbing her pain. Soon she slept.

By the time she awoke, Jove himself had agreed to intercede. He offered Ceres a compromise. Pluto would relinquish her daughter for two-thirds of every year, on the condition that she always return to spend the other months with him. Ceres, hopeful that Proserpine would never go back, assented, and began to nurture the soil once again. Immediately color washed over the fields, flowers burst open, and leaves sprouted on trees. Ceres bathed in the rising brook, spun flax into linen, sewed new garments for the homecoming.

Pluto did not trust solely in the good intentions or devotion of his wife, however. He offered Proserpine a pomegranate before going, knowing that if she partook of the "fruit of the dead" she would be bound to return. Believing that her husband wished only to nourish her for the journey, she bit into his gift, eating heartily. Then she kissed him farewell, her lips pursed with the tart taste of its seeds.

Floating slowly upward, like a diver rising for air, Proserpine tumbled into the flower-laden meadow, her eyes unused to the brilliant sunshine. She had all but forgotten the unbearable sweetness of spring, the thousand colors and scents assailing her from Ceres's bosom. Mother and daughter embraced each other joyfully, their tears falling as April rain. Spring ripened into summer, and summer into autumn, the two content until at last Pluto sent word. Proserpine took leave of the earth reluctantly, borne away on a chill wind. And Ceres let the earth grow cold and barren again until the time of their next reunion, consoling herself, as every year thenceforth, in poppied sleep.

© 1979 Paul Davis

Passion

THE TULIP

The gardens of the seraglio were carpeted with tulips and despair. Ferhad had been advised to make his best effort in preparing the gardens in honor of Ibrahim's state visit to his harem and had devised the most spectacular display of blooms yet seen in the sultan's courtyard. Announcement of the ruler's plans had also caused a flurry of preparations in the secluded quarters of the women, and had thrust Ferhad into the darkest melancholy he had yet suffered in his twenty-four years.

It was not the arduous task ahead of him that troubled the Persian gardener; he welcomed the opportunity to show off his skills. And despite his misery he succeeded in producing so original an effect that even the breath of the sultan was taken away. He used tulips of darkest purple to describe swirling leaf shapes, enclosing within them tulips of red and yellow, striated ones between, the whole creating an immense paisley pattern that undulated in the breeze like the waves of the nearby Bosporus.

Ferhad regarded his achievement with a heavy heart. Picking up a handful of soil, he rubbed the dark clumps into grains, which fell softly through his fingers. He loved this good earth, which rewarded his intimate attentions with an abundance granted few others. It was the occasion for this new display that made him unhappy.

Each tulip evoked the thought of his beloved. He had glimpsed her only once, by miraculous chance, before she vanished into the harem, the "forbidden place," but he could not forget her. Since he did not even know her name, he called her Lalé, reminded by her slender beauty of *lalé,* the almond-shaped wildflowers of his native land, which here in Turkey were *tulipam,* or tulips.

The Turks cultivated the flowers, guarding them as jealously as their women. They named them after the word *tulbend,* for turban, and the sultan liked to think of the rows of tulips as ranks of noblemen, bowing their bulbous heads in obeisance. But to Ferhad they suggested the enslaved women of the seraglio, lovely but powerless, as rooted in the harem as flowers in the earth.

Ferhad had contrived to smuggle a message to Lalé in the Turks' own surreptitious language of love known as *selam,* wherein objects stood for certain rhyming declarations. He sent her a straw, *hasir.* She knew its meaning: *Olim sana yazir,* "Suffer me to be your slave." She responded with a bit of cloth: "Your price is not to be found." He sent a clove: "I have long loved you, and you have not known it." A cake of soap followed: "I am sick with love." Then a pear: "Give me some hope." After a number of agonized days he received from her a coal, *chemur,* meaning *Ben Oliyim size umur,* "May I die, and all my years be yours." He tucked the precious answer into a handkerchief and carried it next to his heart.

But now the sultan was about to hold court among the odalisques. It was inconceivable to the lovesick Ferhad that Ibrahim might fail to notice Lalé, whose image, so fleeting, was inscribed indelibly on his heart. Perhaps the ruler would engage her untried charms at once, although the usual course was to graduate through stages to so coveted a distinction. Ibrahim's licentiousness was rumored within the walls of the seraglio and beyond. Ferhad had heard of harem slaves prancing naked on their hands and knees while the sultan played stallion among them. It was whispered that he stimulated his jaded appetites with mirrors and aphrodisiacs, that he adorned his beard with jewels, and that he looked with special favor on those who proposed inventive scenarios for orgies. There were hints of cruel excesses. Tonight his imaginings tormented him almost past endurance. He pitied his pure Lalé and himself that he might never hold her in his arms.

Ferhad concealed himself in the garden that night, comforted by the tulips with the realization that the sultan could not pay attention to every woman any more than he could take notice of each of the multitude of flowers he had commanded to be planted. Only a few were destined to be chosen to be appreciated individually. His Lalé might be overlooked after all. The gardener fell asleep with hope.

The next morning arrived with gray clouds and a fine cold mist. Ferhad shivered awake. No sounds came from the apartments of the harem. At first he thought he must have slept through the debauch, but something seemed amiss. Alarmed, Ferhad crept along the garden wall, straining for voices. Near the entrance to the eunuchs' quarters he caught snatches of conversation. At first the talk was incomprehensible, but as Ferhad pieced together what he overheard his rage rose like lust. Ibrahim, in a fit of dissatisfaction, had ordered that the entire harem be disposed of before dawn. Three hundred women, groomed solely for his pleasure, had been gagged, tied into sacks weighted with stones, and thrown into the sea, in order that the sultan might have the amusement of replacing them.

The gardener seized his spade, no less a weapon now than a scimitar, and began uprooting the ruler's prized tulips, row by row, until the beds were emptied. Heaping the luckless plants into a huge bundle, he dragged them furiously through the gates onto a promontory. There he flung them, thousands of bright-petaled *lalé*, into the gray-green waters, while fathoms below three hundred corpses swayed like flowers in an underwater garden. Then Ferhad leaped into the Bosporus after his own lost Lalé, her black talisman still pressed to his breast.

Optimism

THE CHRYSANTHEMUM

It was one of those autumn evenings that come unexpectedly after the first frost, a straggling remainder of summer. Akiko lingered in the moon viewing room, envisioning the features of her beloved on the moon's bright face. Then clouds drew across it, their edges glinting with reflected light, until she could imagine him no longer. Smoothing her heavy kimono embroidered with the colors of the season, she moved toward the obscured garden.

She did not change into the wooden sandals meant for garden walking, removing instead her white *tabi* and stepping along the path with bare feet, taking pleasure in the feel of the moss, velvety and damp with dew. Among the twisted pines and tiny maples, the gentle ginkos with fluttering fan-shaped leaves, the stands of bamboo clicking and rustling in the wind, Akiko brooded about her future.

She still was eager to be married, but only to Takeo. Three times she had seen him, each one a formal occasion. They had behaved correctly, bowing deeply to each other, averting their eyes. But there was a genuine attraction between them, and they gladly acceded to the betrothal sought by their families. After their last meeting, Takeo's image had stayed with her constantly, and often made her feel detached from her surroundings. As she prepared for their wedding, she would recite his name with each small task, with each tiny stitch in her sewing. Takeo, Takeo.

Then, without warning, everything had altered. Her fiancé was called into battle. No word of him had reached her for nearly seven years. Her parents, patient at first, urged her to consider other suitors; they were getting old, and she herself was no longer young. But Akiko, in spite of her compliant manner, remained obdurate.

This night she longed for encouragement and, beholding a luminous flower beside a brook, thought to pluck it and consult its petals. But a whispering voice stopped her, or was it only the sound of the water splashing across the stones? "You will have Takeo for your husband," it assured her, "and he will stay with you for as many years as the flower you see has petals." Eight, twenty, fifty petals would not be enough, thought Akiko. She withdrew a long golden pin from her coiffure, and as her black hair fell in cascades she slashed each petal into ribbons, until none was left whole. Then she went to bed.

Akiko had intended to return to the garden by the light of day to see what she had done. But at dawn the very next morning a carriage arrived, sent by Takeo's family to fetch her. Their cryptic request urged her to come at once. Hurriedly she dressed and rode off. When she arrived at Takeo's house, the tear-filled eyes of his parents frightened her. Takeo was alive, they said, but

badly wounded. It was feared he might live only a few more hours. Since he had repeated her name continually during the night, they took the liberty of sending for her without a proper invitation.

In an eight-mat room, Takeo lay upon a soft futon with a small pillow of straw. His face was pale as death and older than she had remembered, but Akiko loved him more than before. Taking his head in her hands, she kissed his eyes and lips and told him that she would never leave his side.

To the astonishment of everyone but Akiko, her fiancé lived through that day, and the next, and began to recover. One day he was well enough to visit her parents' house. As they walked through the garden, Akiko took him to look at her flower. Beside the brook now flourished a moonlike blossom, more luxuriant than any seen before, its countless petals curling in every direction.

The chrysanthemum flower, which the Japanese call *kiku,* is so long-lived and loved that it became the national symbol of Japan. Each year, at the peak of the chrysanthemum season, festivals are held and a toast is still offered: "May the emperor live forever and see the chrysanthemum cup go around autumn after autumn for a thousand years."

Healing

THE PEONY

Had the circumstances of his son's birth not been tragic, or had he himself not been the cause of the tragedy, Apollo might have permitted Aesculapius a more usual education. But conscience dictated that he provide well for the child whom he had virtually orphaned.

Many women had been loved by Apollo. Few upon whom he set his sight could resist such a unity of graces. Young, powerful, agile, he had been suckled on ambrosia and nectar and seemed as sweet. Heavenly musician, brave slayer of monsters, protector of flocks, the son of Zeus supreme, Apollo used as arrows in his bow the very rays of the sun.

One target of his affections had been Coronis, the nubile and beauteous princess of Thessaly. There was a time, alas brief, when he thought himself in love, and pressed her, with a youth's urgency, to give herself to him. Being mortal, she succumbed. By the time she realized she was with child, Apollo had tired of her charms. She married another. Apollo, however, regarded her action as an infidelity, unprovoked, and ordered her put to death. Just as Coronis' body was laid on the funeral pyre, the angry god remembered his unborn child and reached the fire in time to

© 1972 Paul Davis

deliver the infant alive, snatching him from the flames.

Such was the beginning of Aesculapius' life. Apollo put the child into the care of the wise and learned centaur, Chiron, who lived in a cave atop Mount Pelion. Chiron, unlike others of his kind, wild, hybrid creatures with the head and torso of a man and the hindquarters of a horse, had been taught by Apollo himself. Now he was to teach Aesculapius all matters, civilized and wild, known to gods and men.

The boy proved an apt pupil. With the woods and caves of Mount Pelion for his library, Aesculapius learned to forage and hunt. He grew familiar with the needs of flora and fauna, the powers of herbs and venom, the uses of musk and salt tears, and bones. He could extract the secrets of every living thing. So skillful did he become that the gods appointed him their official physician and called him *Paeon,* "the healer."

One day the young doctor happened upon the broken and lifeless body of his friend Hippolytus, who, moments earlier, had been thrown from his chariot and dragged to death by the horses. Aesculapius refused to mourn. Instead he set the splintered bones in place and stitched together the torn flesh. He salved the wounds, applied hot and cold poultices, massaged heart and temples, soles and palms. He recited certain prayers, burned incense, and drew color into the ashen cheeks, moist breath into the dry mouth. As he performed these ministrations, the impossible was accomplished. Hippolytus was returned to life.

What pride Aesculapius felt; what esteem he would bring to his teacher, his father, himself. He anticipated only rewards for his exceptional deed. But Hades, god of the underworld, did not appreciate being cheated. He believed Aesculapius' powers were a threat to his own, and to the natural order of things. He appealed to Zeus for justice, and the supreme god was unable to disagree. Such interference broke the bounds of nature and disrupted the destiny of mortals. From Mount Olympus Zeus loosed a single thunderbolt, which struck Aesculapius dead on the spot.

Apollo, sorely grieved, killed the Cyclopes, the one-eyed giants who had forged the thunderbolts for Zeus, but vengeance did little to assuage his sorrow. Zeus chose to grant him a concession, and instead of delivering Aesculapius' body to Hades, transformed it into the *paeonia,* or peony. The blushing flower was believed to be imbued with Aesculapius' own powers and was prescribed to cure wounds, prevent convulsions, remedy insanity, and ward off evil from that day to this.

Steadfastness

THE CAMELLIA

A lotus exquisitely wrought of gold was offered to the Buddha by a Hindu prince who hoped to hear the Enlightened One preach his philosophy. Accepting it, the Buddha held the golden flower aloft before an assembly of his disciples and said nothing. The silent seminar went on for a long time. At last, one of the disciples, whose attention had not wavered, smiled, and in that smile the holy man recognized that his understanding had passed to the next generation.

Twenty-eight smiles later this enlightenment was received by Bodhidharma, a Buddhist prince from Conjeeveram, near Madras, in India, who possessed exceptional spirit and powers of mind. He was not content, as were his twenty-seven predecessors, to remain in his native land, and, in the sixth century—some say the fifth—took his practice of the *dharma,* or "way," to southern China. There he settled before a stone wall. It was his intention to meditate in that place for seven years—some say nine—without sleeping at all.

Night followed upon night. Stars pierced the blackness or did not, the moon shone or did not, the air turned sharp and cold or did not. He sat, as he had grown accustomed to do, under a

35

gnarled tree, always facing the wall. When snow fell on his shoulders, hair, and eyelashes, Ta-mo, as the Chinese called their mystifying foreigner, neither shivered nor blinked. In this manner he sat through the seasons until they had come and gone several times.

Ta-mo's endeavor was talked about far and wide. It was unnatural, a man staying awake for years on end. Who would have thought it was even possible? Some of the curious ridiculed him. Others shrugged. A few remained to pray at his feet, this fierce, dignified mendicant, implacably gazing at something no one else could see.

Meditation was not unknown in China at that time. Old Indian texts on yoga had long been translated into the language, and seekers had experimented with such practices as were described. But Ta-mo's meditation was not a complement to his philosophy. It was its very essence, "a direct pointing at the soul." In demonstration of this he sat, day into night, week into month, year into years. His eyes never closed.

Word of Ta-mo's conduct reached the emperor, who summoned him at once to the capital. The ruler, proud of his own works in the service of their mutual faith, described to his guest the acts of his dedication. He told of the great temples and monasteries he had commanded to be built, and of his generous support of monks and nuns. He exhibited the sacred books of the Buddha that he had copied painstakingly in his own hand. "What do you think of my worthiness?" the emperor inquired of Ta-mo. "Nothing, your

Paul Davis © 1979

majesty," replied the sage. The stunned monarch demanded an explanation. "These are but worldly deeds," Ta-mo answered. "They are like the shadows that fall from objects, their substance but an illusion. Truly worthy deeds are beyond human appreciation, being both perfect and mysterious, hidden from rational understanding."

The emperor's practical mind would not yield. He asked Ta-mo to recite the first principle of his holy doctrine. "Vast emptiness," said the patriarch, "and there is nothing holy in it." "Well, then, whom do I address?" challenged the emperor in confusion. "I have no idea," concluded Ta-mo, and returned to his meditation under the tree.

More years went by. It seemed that Ta-mo was not to be subject to the failures of will or flesh as other human beings. He himself may have begun, unwittingly, to believe so. One summer evening, like countless others, the sky swelled with thick clouds. Insects droned hypnotically in the still air. Ta-mo's eyelids lowered imperceptibly, just a fraction, and they did so again the next night, and the night after that, until one night they lay completely unfolded against his weary eyes. He slept—some say for a moment, some say for a year. When he awoke he was horrified at his weakness. Springing instantly to his feet, Ta-mo drew his sword from his side and with razor swiftness sliced the offending lids from his eyes. They fell to the ground, and trickles of blood ran down his cheeks like tears.

It is said that the Buddha felt such compassion for the twenty-eighth bearer of his enlightened smile that he caused the severed lids to take root, and in their place to arise a flowering bush of unsurpassed beauty, with leaves curved like eyelids. Ta-mo boiled the leaves, poured the aromatic brew into a bowl and proffered it to visitors who gathered, afterward drinking of it himself. This, the first tea of the first camellia plant on earth, banished his fatigue and sustained him to the end of his vigil.

There is no certain record of what happened after. Bodhidharma was reported variously to have been poisoned by rivals, to have crossed the desert back to India, and to have carried his faith onward to Japan. Accounts agree, however, that he exceeded one hundred fifty years at the time of his death.

© 1979 Paul Davis

Eloquence

THE IRIS

Tens of centuries before the first riddles were posed, before the great pyramids were set upon the sand, when rains still watered the land and made it green, it is said that spirits walked among the people and Ra, god of the Egyptian sun, ruled heaven and earth by the power of his secret name. The name had brought Ra and the universe into being, and he guarded its knowledge with all his might, for whoever could learn it, human or divine, would acquire sovereignty over the world, and even over Ra himself.

The goddess Isis also lived on earth and possessed words of magic of her own, but still she envied the superior powers of Ra. As she watched him daily rising onto his eastern throne, crossing through the sky in his boat of incomparable majesty, and retiring in the west each night, she yearned to subjugate him. But her charms and spells were useless.

The sun god grew old. So many millions of times had he traveled over the world that fatigue finally overtook him. One evening, as he neared the earth, Isis saw saliva trickle from a corner of his mouth and fall upon the ground. Ever watchful for an opportunity, she scooped up the bit of spittled dust and molded it into a small hooded snake with fangs of poison. Setting the creature in Ra's path near the western throne, she waited without need of charms or spells, since her weapon contained the god's own substance.

The next evening, as Ra approached the far horizon, he failed to notice the serpent, perhaps mistaking it for a harmless flower, the iris, which it resembled. As the creature struck, its fangs darted deeply into the great god's flesh. Ra shrieked in pain, his cries resounding through the heavens. Men and gods shuddered at the terrible sound. "What is wrong? What afflicts thee?" questioned his retainers, but Ra could muster no reply. His teeth chattered, his body shook, and the poison overran him as the Nile overruns its banks in the season of rains.

When he collected some strength, Ra spoke. "Come to me, ye gods whom I have created, and I will tell what awful thing has happened. Something deadly has wounded me, something I have neither seen nor made. Who is it in the universe that has the power to hurt me thus? No one knows the name buried within my breast, kept secret so that no magic could touch me. Let all who have healing powers now come forth."

Among the listeners was Isis, sorceress of words, whose breath could resurrect the dead. Feigning ignorance, the goddess stepped forward. "Oh, divine father," she said, "I can try to overcome by my own poor words of magic whatever has dared lift its head against thee. But I know with certainty that I can vanquish it with thine own invincible force." In a soothing voice Isis asked Ra to reveal to her, and her alone, his true and secret name, "for who is called by his name," she promised, "must live."

"I am the maker of heaven and earth," answered Ra slowly. "I am the builder of mountains, and all that live upon them. I am the inventor of love and its ecstasies. I am he who brings light with the opening of his eyes and darkness with the closing of them. I am the creator of the hours and the days, who makes the waters run in the rivers and life through men's veins."

"Thy works are without equal," Isis agreed. "But thou hast not spoken thy name."

"I am called Khepri in the morning, Ra at noon, Atum at night," the god of the sun replied.

"These names are already known," answered Isis, "but still thou hast not spoken thy true and secret name. My magic can work only on those whose names I know," she explained. "Do not be afraid. Tell me thy true and secret name."

The poison continued to spread and to burn fiercely inside the body of Ra like the sun's own fire. He allowed Isis to search his breast and his name to pass into her, and he agreed further to give the sun and moon to her blind son Horus for eyes. Her dearest ambitions achieved, the goddess then commanded, "Ra shall live and the poison shall die." Thus Ra was healed by the strength of his name, but he ruled alone no longer, and the boat of the sun floated empty in the Egyptian sky.

In the Egyptian desert the sun at dawn looms abruptly, a great orange disk shimmering on the horizon. As it ascends into the sky, it grows smaller and a shadow falls across the face of the Sphinx, cast by an ornament above its inscrutable brow. The form is that of the divine cobra, once worshiped as an incarnation of the sun-god himself, but there are those who see in it an iris, a flower whose roots were believed to possess curative powers and which was known to signify the power of words.

Sincerity

THE LILY

King Konetos suspected that his daughter was remarkable from the very hour of her birth. Even as a babe Catherine's eyes shone with intelligence, and she transfixed people with her clear and earnest gaze. Superintending her studies, he was not disappointed in his expectations of her; by ten years of age she was fluent in both Greek and Hebrew, and by twelve in Latin and Aramaic as well. At fifteen she understood the epicyclic rotations of the heavenly bodies according to Ptolemy, and had mastered geometry and geography, literature and philosophy. In fourth-century Alexandria, where women were routinely well educated, Catherine's gifts were acknowledged as exceptional. She was also very beautiful. Konetos could not help but be proud as he watched her flowering.

At eighteen Catherine converted to Christianity, after the Virgin appeared to her in a dream, and for the first time in her life gave her father serious cause for concern. All her estimable powers of persuasion were devoted to proselytizing, and although most of those who argued ultimately accepted her views, tension grew between father and daughter as Konetos resisted her tireless efforts to convert him. The governing Roman emperor, Max-

© 1979 Paul Davis

iminus, had recently renewed the harsh persecution of Christians in Egypt, and Konetos feared not only for the safety of Catherine and his subjects but for his own position as well. He hoped for both their sakes that his daughter would give up her obsession. He still hoped she would marry, bear children, and fulfill the happy ambitions he held for her future.

But Catherine not only persisted in preaching her beliefs, she demanded an audience with Maximinus himself, daring to upbraid him to his face for his cruelties and worship of idols. The emperor was hardly accustomed to such audacity, especially from a woman, and the affront combined with the virtues of one so young and beautiful conspired to make the emperor fall in love. He ignored the issues she raised and proposed marriage instead.

Konetos begged her to accept. His daughter would be the most powerful woman in Alexandria. It was a position befitting her talents, and more wonderful than even he had dared to dream. But Catherine would not hear of it, and she continued to preach to all who would listen. Maximinus rejected and enraged, summoned fifty philosophers to refute her arguments. When they failed, he had them burned alive. He condemned her to torture on a spiked wheel to force her to recant; the instrument of torture flew into splinters at her touch. Two hundred Roman soldiers sent to guard her were converted, and Maximinus ordered them beheaded. Finally, he ordered Catherine beheaded, too. The executioner reported that milk, not blood, flowed from her veins.

Konetos, upon learning of the death of his dear child, fell into a swoon. He dreamed that he and Catherine were walking together as in earlier days. As she put forth her proofs yet again, they reached a fork in the road. To the left ran a path smooth and wide, inviting him into a green valley, but when he was halfway down he realized that Catherine was no longer with him. He looked up and saw that she had chosen the other path, steep and rocky, winding precipitously around a mountain whose peak was enshrouded in fog. She looked back at him and beckoned, and then was lost from sight.

An irresistible fragrance drew the king in Catherine's direction. It grew stronger as he gained the summit, where he was met by a dazzling sight. There, in a field of white lilies, his Catherine stood in betrothal to Christ. Blinded by her radiance, he fell to his knees, trembling, renouncing his false gods and vowing to become a Christian. Catherine helped him to his feet and gently ushered him through a golden gate.

Waking in the brilliant sunlight, Konetos found himself utterly calm and at peace, all grief gone. From that day forth, he filled his house with lilies, which were believed to have had no fragrance before that time. Their perfume comforted him and sustained his faith until the end of his days.

Wisdom

THE LOTUS

The pond lay still in the vanishing mist, a mirror to the dawn. The first rays of the sun flashed through the trees, and a lotus, as if signaled, rose from nocturnal sleep below to break the glassy surface. Concentric circles rippled outward from it to the shore.

The delicate disturbance awakened tiny insects who lived on the pond. Some of them darted off at once in search of a meal, but others regarded the flower inquisitively as it opened its cleanly washed petals to the new day. The lotus held a troubling mystery for the tiny denizens of the pond. Every so often one of their number would swim to it, climb upon it, and vanish, never to be seen again.

This morning, the urge to inspect the lotus overpowered one of them, who, having confessed her intention to her companions, promised faithfully to return and report what had befallen the others. Then she struck out bravely across the water.

The distance was farther than it had first appeared. By the time she reached the base of the lotus, the sun was overhead. Nearly exhausted, she used her remaining strength to make the slippery ascent up the petals. At the rim of the flower's cup she lost her balance and toppled in, her heart pounding with terror, but once inside the silvery crater found nothing to fear and soon relaxed in the sun's warmth. At last she stretched herself, and an odd thing happened. Her shell, her inseparable armor, began to crack. As it fell away, panic arose, then subsided; she was vulnerable, but she was also free.

She beheld herself with astonishment. Wings, iridescent with rainbows, sprouted from either side of her denuded body. She tried fluttering them, cautiously, then with more confidence, lifting herself just a little at first, then higher and higher, up past the edge of the lotus, up into the sky, until she could survey the entire pond at once. There were her companions, still looking for her in the direction of the lotus. She hovered over them, trying to attract their attention, to tell them what she had learned. But they were wary of this glossy intruder.

Then she understood. They could not recognize her. They would never believe it was she, who only that morning had been like them. Ah, she realized, they will have to find out for themselves. And spreading her wings, she flew away into the waiting afternoon.

© 1979 Paul Davis